DISCARDED
TELFORD & WREKIN LIBRARIES

TE

Please return/renew this item
by the last date shown.
Items may also be renewed by
Telephone and Internet.
Telford & Wrekin Libraries
www.telford.gov.uk/libraries

Palmer said so!' **??**

D1513068

More great reads in the SHADES 2.0 series:

The
CALLING

Penny Bates

Ransom

TELFORD & WREKIN LIBRARIES	
Bertrams	21/10/2014
HOS	£5.99

SHADES 2.0
The Calling
by Penny Bates

Published by Ransom Publishing Ltd.
Radley House, 8 St. Cross Road, Winchester, Hampshire SO23 9HX, UK
www.ransom.co.uk

ISBN   978 178127 634 1
First published in 2014

Copyright © 2014 Ransom Publishing Ltd.
Text copyright © 2014 Penny Bates
Cover photograph copyright © Clint Spencer

A CIP catalogue record of this book is available from the British Library.

All rights reserved. No part of this publication may be reproduced, stored in a
retrieval system, or transmitted, in any form or by any means, electronic, mechanical,
photocopying, recording or otherwise, without the prior permission of the
publishers.

The right of Penny Bates to be identified as the author of this Work has been
asserted by her in accordance with sections 77 and 78 of the Copyright, Design and
Patents Act 1988.

CONTENTS

Dragon House blinked open its shutters in the breeze and sighed deeply. Sunshine smiled on its gloomy face. The cracked windows frowned back. The roof sagged as light crept over the broken tiles.

At eight o'clock in the morning, the boiler belched and the radiators spat out heat into the empty rooms. An icy chill slid down the stairs. The walls shivered as they clung to their blanket of paint. Pale yellow, painted blue then washed over with grey. Now the colour was slimy green with spots of mould.

The house had seen many people come and go. Once there were babies for the house to care for. Families had been and gone. There were farm workers and gardeners. Teachers and nurses followed cooks and cleaners. The house looked after them all, as their lives grew busy and time slipped away.

Dragon House had been lived in and loved for a hundred years. It stood on top of a hill surrounded by fields. Today there were sheep in the fields and daffodils spilling through the gate, as there had always been.

There were birds in the old apple tree

and tadpoles in the pond. A cat sat in a patch of sunlight watching the fish. Some things had never changed, like the house itself.

No one ever wanted to alter the windows at Dragon House, or knock down walls. No one ever talked about building extra rooms, and the house was glad.

The people who lived in Dragon House loved the place just as it was, like the old woman who had lived there for the last twenty years. She lived and died there peacefully, as she always wanted.

'This house has lived and breathed for a hundred years,' Grace Palmer told visitors. 'If you listen carefully, you'll hear its heartbeat.'

TWO

Now there was sadness in the house. It had watched Grace leave for the last time in the cheap coffin ordered by her son. It saw the estate agent arrive the same day with the 'For Sale' sign.

'This place should fetch a good price,' the estate agent told Grace's son. 'It's a wreck, but I think a builder will buy it. It's easy to bring these old places up to date if you know how. I'd tear out the floors, ceilings – the lot!'

The building's heart missed a beat. Grace's son smiled at the thought of the money from Dragon House. The estate agent grinned. Then the house shuddered as he scraped a finger down its front door.

'This paint has seen better days,' the estate agent added. 'But a builder will soon strip this place back to its bare walls.'

The house shook as the 'For Sale' sign was hammered into place. A tile rattled and smashed onto the ground. The cat turned and ran. The birds flew into the sky. But there was nowhere for the house to go.

Its heart started to beat faster at the thought of what was to come. The stripping and the smashing. The pounding and the pushing. Then fear turned to anger as

Grace's son slammed shut the front door and trod a cigarette butt into the step.

'The old girl will turn in her grave when the builders arrive!' he laughed. 'She wanted me to move in and keep the house just as it is!'

A pane of glass cracked in the dark red door as Dragon House shook with rage. It spat and roared at the two men as they slammed shut the garden gate. The foundations shook. Walls cracked.

The Dragon was awake.

'Look at that dust coming out through the tiles,' the estate agent said. 'Anyone would think the house was on fire!'

'The old girl was never keen on housework,' Grace's son replied. 'The house is held together by cobwebs!'

Dragon House fumed silently. In a few weeks' time there would be men in yellow helmets smashing down its walls. They would bring pick axes and drills, hammers and chisels. Glass would be shattered and timbers stripped.

The house gave an angry sigh. It had to strike back.

'The wind must be getting up!' the estate agent said, as the house's shutters started to creak backwards and forwards on their rusty hinges. 'Let's lock the shutters to stop that creepy noise!'

'Leave them,' muttered Grace's son as the shutters flapped slowly like giant wings. 'It's time for a beer.'

There was no wind. Only the sound of Dragon House beating its bony wings. Waking the dead.

The house was calling them home.

THREE

Anna Martin frowned as her mother pushed open the dark red door to Dragon House.

'Home, sweet home!' Kate Martin said with a smile, as she led Anna inside. 'I know you'll just love it.'

Anna sighed when she saw the narrow hallway with its dusty floorboards. She poked her foot at some plaster that had fallen from the walls.

'It's a mess, Mum!' Anna moaned. 'I wish you'd have let me see this before you bought it. After all, I've got to live here too! And it'll mean yet another school. I'm the only fifteen-year-old I know who's had to move house three times in as many years!'

'This is how I make a living!' Kate Martin snapped back. 'I make lots of money turning old wrecks into palaces and selling them on. That's why I can afford to buy you designer clothes.'

Anna bit her lip. There was no point arguing. She had told her mother that she did not need designer clothes to be happy. She had begged her mother to let her stay in the same school with the same group of friends. But it was not to be. Kate Martin had big plans for Dragon House.

Kate cast an expert eye on walls and windows as she showed Anna around the house.

'It won't take long to knock the plaster off all the downstairs rooms,' Kate said, as they climbed the wooden staircase. 'And I'm thinking of knocking out the brickwork from under the stairs to make the kitchen bigger.'

There was a shudder in the stairs as Kate spoke, and Anna reached quickly for the handrail.

'Did you feel that?' Anna gasped as she tried to steady herself. 'I thought the stairs were about to give way!'

'Just a bit of dry rot,' Kate replied.

'But it's an old ruin, Mum!' Anna said, as they stumbled across the shabby carpet on the landing. 'And it smells of mothballs and little old ladies!'

'Of course it does!' Kate laughed. 'I always wanted a little old lady's house, because she wouldn't have modernised it. There are some lovely old features here. The oak panels in the dining room will be a big selling point.'

Anna crept out of the house as soon as her mother's back was turned. She stared back at the cracked glass in the red door and wanted to cry. This wasn't home at all. It was just another empty shell to be filled with noisy workmen.

Her mother was on the phone right now, hiring builders and plumbers. There would be electricians too, and endless groups of men wanting cups of tea. The tea-making was always Anna's job and she hated it.

'I'll never pass any exams at this rate,' Anna said out loud. 'I'll never catch up when I start at the new school!'

'Life can't be so bad, dear,' said the voice behind the garden gate. 'You're so lucky to be living at Dragon House.'

The old woman's eyes sparkled as she watched Anna walk towards her. She held out a wrinkled hand that smelt of mothballs. Anna shivered in the sunshine and took a step back.

The woman was smiling and yet there was a cold look in her pale face and stone grey eyes.

'This house has lived and breathed a hundred years,' the old woman began. 'If you listen carefully, you'll hear its heartbeat.'

FOUR

'You must be Anna,' the old woman said, as she stared back at the house.

Anna felt her fingers turn to ice as they shook hands. There was no flesh beneath the old woman's grip. Only skin and bones.

'You'll be nice and warm in Dragon House when winter comes,' the woman added with a smile. 'Such a cosy place. And in the autumn you'll see the creeper on the walls turn bright red, as if the Dragon's breathing fire!

'Summer's the best time, though. There'll be flowers like bright yellow flames.'

'I don't think we'll be here to see all the seasons,' Anna replied sadly. 'Mum buys and sells houses. She does them up and then we move on.'

'That's a shame,' the old lady said. 'I hoped you'd be able to look after my cat. Have you spotted him in the garden yet? He usually sits by the pond. I wanted to take Sam with me, but I couldn't.'

Anna saw a tear in the woman's eye.

'So you used to live here?' Anna asked gently. 'Where do you live now?'

'Let's just say I've passed on, my dear,' came the reply. 'And there's no room for cats.'

Anna felt cross. It wasn't fair when old people had to go into nursing homes where they couldn't have pets.

'Don't worry about Sam,' Anna said kindly. 'I'll look after him for as long as we're here. I might be able to get Mum to agree to keep him. I've always wanted a cat.'

'Well that's a weight off my mind,' the old woman said. 'But I hope you'll look after the house too. It's not a house to be messed with. Tell your mother that it doesn't like change. It's better to let the Dragon sleep, my dear. I don't want a girl like you to come to any … '

Anna looked away when she felt the brush of fur against her leg. A striped cat purred loudly as it twisted and turned around Anna's ankles.

'Nice to meet you, Sam!' Anna laughed

as she stroked the cat from head to tail. Its fur was soft and warm. 'You and I will get on just fine!'

When Anna looked up, the old woman had gone.

FIVE

'Why are people never around when you need them?' Kate Martin snapped. Anna walked into the front room with Sam in her arms. 'There's all this plaster to chip off and I can't do everything myself! And where on Earth has that cat come from?'

The room was old-fashioned, with its low ceiling and tiny windows. There was a huge fireplace with tiles all round. In winter there would be burning logs and dancing yellow flames. Now the wood basket was empty.

Sam sat by the fireplace in his usual place.

'I'll help as long as I can keep Sam,' Anna insisted. 'I've decided I'm going to like it here. I know it's shabby round the edges, but all it needs is some love.'

'You've changed your tune!' Kate said. 'But remember we'll be moving as soon as the work is finished. Don't start getting fond of the place!'

Anna made her mother a cup of tea and told her about the old woman.

'Country people always have to poke their noses in,' Kate said. 'Time and time again I've heard them say that nothing must change. Well I've got a living to make and I don't care what some busybody thinks about Dragon House.

'That woman can't have lived here, because the estate agent said the last owner was dead! And what a cheek, asking you to take in a stray cat. I bet your new *friend* must have dumped it here!'

The tea tray rattled on the floor as a shiver of rage ran through the floorboards. A china cup trembled in its saucer until the movement stopped.

'Wood rot, no doubt!' Kate said as she wiped spots of spilt tea. 'The builders will soon rip those timbers out.'

'But the old lady said you can hear the house's heartbeat!' Anna said, as she watched Sam's eyes stare hard at the floor as if it were alive. 'She said it lives and breathes like a sleeping dragon. And she *wasn't* a busybody. I think she was trying to warn us!'

'Trying to warn us off, no doubt!' Kate laughed. 'I got this house at a bargain price and I'm going to make a good profit. I bet your friend wanted the place for herself.'

There was a scratching beneath the floorboards, like a scraping of claws. The shutters on the windows slammed shut. Sam gave a loud hiss and ran from the room.

'It sounds like we've got rats, too!' Kate said, as she saw the fear on Anna's face. 'Rats and a useless cat!'

'Great timing, Mum!' Anna said, as the builder's van pulled up outside Dragon House. 'My first day at the new school and I won't even be able to eat breakfast in peace because *they're* here already!'

There was a blast of music as the van's doors swung open. Then the heavy boots of Morris and Sons crashed towards the front door. The house shook itself awake as a fist smashed into the red paint.

'Morning, Mrs Martin,' boomed a cheerful voice, as Anna's mother opened the door. 'We'll start early before it gets too warm. Knocking down walls is sticky work.'

'Gives you a throat as dry as the desert,' chipped in a smaller man with a cigarette glued to his lips.

'Any chance of a cuppa?' said a third man, as he pushed himself into the hallway with a bag of tools.

Anna muttered something her mother wished she hadn't heard as the men made their way into the kitchen.

'Not enough room to swing a cat in 'ere!' the man with the booming voice said, as Sam bolted away. 'I can see why you want an extension. First job will be to knock out those bricks from under the stairs … '

Then Anna decided to grab her school things and bolt too.

'Bye, Mum!' she called above the noise as the builders turned up their radio. 'I'll grab some breakfast on the way to school.'

Sam was hiding under a bush by the garden gate as Anna ran towards it to make her escape. She stopped when she saw his shivering fur and lifted him up.

'Poor Sam,' she whispered. 'I'm just as scared as you. You're scared of the builders and I'm scared of going to that new school.'

She stroked the side of Sam's face until he began to purr.

'Don't worry, Sam. I won't let those builders hurt you. I just wish Mum wanted to take care of me. She could have wished me good luck!'

'Your mother's a silly woman!' said the voice behind the gate. 'There's more to life than making money. And there's more to death, too!'

Anna shivered in spite of the early morning sunshine. A smell of mothballs filled the air.

'But *you* know that, Anna,' the old woman said, gripping the gate with strong, bony hands. 'Tell that mother of yours she's playing with fire. This building work must not start. Tell her that Grace Palmer said so!'

There was anger in the woman's stone grey eyes. An icy stare. Anna felt the ice creep inside her and slither down her spine.

'Mum doesn't mean any harm,' Anna replied. 'But I know some people don't like change.'

The old woman knelt down and reached out her hand to Sam. The cat crouched down low and hissed softly, as if frightened by a dog.

'So you *can* see me after all, Sam,' the old woman said strangely. 'Too cold for you, am I?'

'It's not your fault that you couldn't take Sam to the nursing home,' Anna said. 'Why are there such stupid rules?'

The old woman nodded towards the house as the sound of hammering smashed across the garden. She gripped the gate again, as if in pain.

'There are rules in this world and the next, Anna,' the woman said sadly. 'You're a good girl, and I'm sorry for what's to come. But now the house has started to call us home, there can be no turning back.'

A drill screeched in the distance. The shutters crashed against the walls without the help of wind. The ground rumbled beneath Anna's feet, as if a huge beast was growling with rage.

'They've hurt it now!' the old woman cried out as she walked away. 'Shoved a stake into its heart. Take Sam with you, Anna. Don't come back.'

SEVEN

'My head's pounding!' Kate groaned when Anna came home from school. 'Perhaps I'm getting too old for all this.'

Anna wondered how long it would take for her mother to ask about her day at school. It hadn't been a good day. There were too many stares as she walked into classrooms and giggles behind her back.

'I really can't make up my mind about the cupboards for the new kitchen.' Kate sighed as she reached for the pile of catalogues stacked by the fireplace. 'Perhaps pine would be best.'

Anna unpacked her school bag. Surely her mother would ask about school now?

'And speaking of wood, I must order some logs for the fire. I know it's meant to be spring, but this place always seems cold. A good fire will help the new plaster in the kitchen to dry. Then I'll need your help with some painting … '

Anna kicked her feet as she held back the tears. No one had spoken to her today, apart from the teachers. No one had tried to be her friend. No one cared about the new girl. Not even her mother.

'Watch where you put your feet!' Kate snapped. 'I don't want dirty marks on those curtain samples.'

Anna looked crossly at the floor. Sometimes her mother could be so untidy. There was a heap of fabric thrown beside the catalogues. Faded photographs spilled out from an envelope on a pile of papers.

'What's the point of buying logs if we can't even get close to the fireplace!' Anna sighed crossly. 'And if those photos are important, I'd keep them away from the rest of the rubbish.'

'Oh I don't care about those!' Kate replied. 'They can be thrown away. Just another busybody writing to say he used to live here. He's sent photos to show how the house looked in his day.'

Anna picked up the photographs and a letter from someone called Eric Bailey.

'Mr Bailey says he lived in Dragon House in the 1960s. He used to be a teacher, but now he's retired. Have you looked at these photos, Mum? The house looks just the same as it does today.'

Kate snatched the photos and threw them back on the floor. The paper and fabric crept closer to the fireplace.

'As I said, these can be thrown away. What a nerve that man has, telling me what to do! *Nothing must change*, he says. It's none of his business!'

Anna shuddered. It really was cold in the room now, and suddenly the worries about school didn't seem so important. Now only Dragon House was dark and scary in her mind.

'But that's exactly what Grace Palmer said!' Anna said, wanting her mother to hear. 'I saw her again this morning and she said the building work must not start. Then she heard the builders and said something really strange. She said that the house had called her home and it was calling the others too!'

Kate frowned but quickly changed the subject.

'Remind me to order those logs.'

'Please listen, Mum!' Anna begged. 'I don't think it's safe here. Grace told me not to come home.'

'I've heard just about enough of this!' Kate snapped. 'I went to town yesterday to check the deeds because of the building work. Someone called Grace Palmer did live here before us, but now she's moved on.'

'I knew it!' Anna said. 'I didn't think she was lying. But where does she live now? It can't be far away and it'd be nice to go and see her. Then she can talk to you about the house.'

'You can go if you want,' Kate replied angrily. 'You'll find her buried in the churchyard!'

EIGHT

Anna couldn't sleep. There were too many things to think about. Too many fears clawing at her mind. How could Grace be dead? She was old, but her voice was strong. She cared about Dragon House, but said it was a place of danger.

Anna bit her lip as she remembered Grace's words. They were words of warning.

Wasn't that what ghosts set out to do? They warned the living of dangers to come. And who were the people the house was calling home?

There were too many questions. Anna slipped out of bed and went downstairs to make some hot chocolate. It was school again in the morning, and she knew she had to sleep somehow.

The house was quiet as she crept downstairs. She switched on the kitchen light and smiled at Sam, who was twitching as he slept.

'Are you dreaming, Sam?' Anna whispered as she opened the fridge door.

The cat woke with a wide-eyed stare. He got up and went straight to the front door. Anna followed.

'Sam, it's only me!' Anna said softly. 'There's no need to be scared.'

Then Anna heard the noise. It was a soft scratching at first, like a tiny mouse. It came from beneath the floorboards. Anna bent her head to one side to listen. Then the scratching grew louder and sharper. *Not a mouse*, Anna thought. Mice didn't have claws.

Sam howled to go out and Anna unlocked the door. She stepped outside in the moonlight and stared back at the house. The two outside lamps loomed large in the darkness, like a reptile's golden eyes. The roof tiles shimmered in the moonlight like the scales of an enormous lizard.

Then the claws reached out again from inside the house and Anna shuddered at the sound. It was as if someone had dragged fingernails across a blackboard. There was something moving beneath the floorboards. Something dragging itself towards her.

Anna wanted to run, but her feet stood firm. Whatever was moving in the darkness she knew she had to stay. She had to understand.

The door slammed shut behind her like a snapping jaw. Anna's heart missed a beat. Then she remembered what Grace said about Dragon House.

'If you listen carefully you'll hear its heartbeat.'

Anna looked out across the garden and listened. An owl hooted in the darkness and leaves fluttered in the breeze. The moon shone down on Anna's pale face. Blood drummed in her ears as her own heart pounded in fear. Then the deep, throbbing sound began. The beat of the Dragon's heart.

'So you really are alive,' Anna whispered.

'The people just come and go, but you are always here. You watch over the garden and the fields. You breathe the same air that I breathe. You feel pain like I do. Please forgive Mum. She doesn't understand that she's hurting you!'

Grace's words returned to give the Dragon's answer.

'There can be no turning back!'

A cloud crossed the moon and cut out the light. A low growl rumbled beneath the earth. Anna hugged herself for warmth as Grace suddenly appeared beside her.

'You've worked it out, Anna,' the old woman said as she reached out her hand. 'The house is alive. I'm dead.'

NINE

The Dragon burned in Anna's head all
night. It spat lightning and rocked her
world with a roar like thunder. She could
not rest, but spent the night huddled in
the garden shed with Sam. She could only
face going back into the house when
daylight came.

'You're up early,' Kate said, as Anna

came into the kitchen.

There were black marks under Anna's eyes, but her mother didn't notice. There was a look of frozen fear in Anna's face.

'Mum, we have to leave!' Anna begged, as she tugged Kate by the hand. 'Dragon House is alive. The old woman said so, and last night I knew it was true.'

Kate sighed as she pulled her hand from Anna's grip.

'I didn't think fifteen year olds believed in fairy tales,' Kate said. 'Why bother telling tales about Grace Palmer when we both know she's dead?'

There was a knock on the door before Anna could reply. A rush of cold air filled the hallway as Kate opened the door. Anna could feel the chill creep round her ankles as she stood by the kitchen table.

'I thought you'd be needing some help in

the garden,' Anna heard the man's voice say. 'Takes a lot of work, this garden. And I should know, because I lived here once. I'm Fred Dean.'

Anna pulled up the collar on her dressing gown as she peered around the kitchen door.

The man left a trail of straw and dry leaves on the floor as Kate showed him into the front room.

'It's a bit early, I know,' the man explained. 'I work at the farm, you see, so I thought I'd call in when I was passing … '

'It's kind of you to offer to help, Mr Dean, but I don't need a gardener,' Anna heard her mother reply. 'Most of the garden will disappear when the house is extended.'

'That's a shame,' the man said quietly. 'When Eric Bailey was alive he spent all his free time making a beautiful garden. He planted the daffodils and made the pond. I bought Dragon House because I fell in love with the garden. It's sad to think the garden has to die like the rest of us … '

Anna heard her mother say a firm goodbye as she closed the front door. The cold air clung to Anna's skin and she could see that her mother was shivering. Now Anna was shaking too.

'Another do-gooder trying to tell me what to do!' Kate said angrily. 'And he's made such a mess by the fireplace. There's straw everywhere!'

'When Eric Bailey was *alive* … ' Anna whispered. 'Don't you see? Eric Bailey's letter said that nothing must change.'

'And I certainly won't be listening to him!' Kate muttered.

'No you won't, Mum,' Anna snapped back. 'That's just my point. Your letter came from a dead man!'

TEN

'They'll burn brightly,' said the farmer delivering the logs. 'They're good and dry. You can't beat apple wood for a real blaze. There's a nice bit of oak, too.'

Kate smiled. At last things seemed to be going well. The builders were hard at work and Anna had gone to school without a word about dead people. It was so hard to convince her that the letter from Eric Bailey had to be a joke.

'It's kind of you to bring the wood,' Kate said, as the man filled the log basket by the fire. 'You must have read my mind, because I was going to order some logs today.'

'Fred Dean said you'd be wanting some wood,' the man replied. 'It always did get cold in this house, even in late spring.'

'You're right,' Kate added, zipping up her thick cardigan. 'I can feel the cold even now!'

The man stacked the logs by the side of the fire. He stepped carefully over the pile of catalogues and old letters left by the fireplace. He pushed the faded photographs towards the wood basket to avoid treading on them, and laughed when he saw the pile of straw and leaves left behind by Fred Dean.

'You can always tell where Fred's been,' he said. 'I call him a walking scarecrow.'

'I suppose I'm not always tidy myself,' Kate answered. 'I've been meaning to clear away all that rubbish for weeks.'

The farmer smiled as he picked up one of Eric Bailey's old photographs.

'To think I used to stay here when I was a kid. Eric Bailey was my uncle. He loved his garden. And I loved to stay in Dragon House when I came to visit. It always felt like the house was keeping me safe.

'Once you live here, it's in your blood. And it's in your heart when your blood runs dry.'

There was no warmth in the farmer's skin when he shook Kate's hand. No blood running through his flesh.

'Goodbye, Mrs Martin,' he called as he left Dragon House. 'Think of me when you're roasting in front of that nice, roaring fire.'

ELEVEN

Dragon House sighed deeply as it watched the sunset through the trees for the very last time. It had lived and breathed for a hundred years, and now it was time to die.

The Dragon growled softly as the sky burned pink and gold.

There was beauty in fire. Power.

As the sun sank behind the clouds, the

Dragon House knew there would be no more warmth pouring through its windows. No more people to care for. Better to die in flames than to be slowly eaten away by hammers and chisels.

Now the calling was over. The Dragon had woken the dead and brought them home.

The old woman came first. The dead man sent his letter. Then the gardener and the farmer completed the plan.

Together they could bring fire back into the Dragon's belly. Together they would help the Dragon to die.

Dragon House watched as the woman and her daughter came back from a walk on the hillside. A striped cat followed them. Soon they would go inside and draw the curtains. Then they would lock the doors.

The fire was already laid.

TWELVE

'I'm so tired!' Kate yawned, as she opened the front door to Dragon House. 'That was a long walk.'

'I think Sam's worn out too,' Anna replied, as she slipped off her muddy shoes. 'Fancy him following us all the way!'

Sam led the way into the front room and sat by the fireplace. He started to play with the trail of straw and torn photographs on the floor.

'Sam seems wide awake to me!' Kate laughed. 'But I'm too tired to clear up that mess tonight. I'll tidy up tomorrow.'

Kate took off her coat and knelt by the fireplace. She reached for a box of matches.

'I laid the fire this morning,' she said, as she lit the paper and twigs beneath the logs. 'I thought it'd be nice to have our supper in front of a roaring fire.'

The fire crackled into life. Anna held out her hands to the warmth of the flames. Her face was pink from the effort of the long walk, but she still felt strangely cold. Sam rubbed around her knees as she watched the logs spark orange and yellow.

The fire was burning brightly, but the heat did not reach her. There was a chill in the house that could not be warmed.

'This will keep out the cold!' Kate said, bringing two steaming plates of stew from the kitchen.

Anna shivered as she ate her meal by the fire. She pushed her food from side to side, knowing something was wrong. The Dragon had been strangely quiet all day. The builders had been drilling and yet there had been no snarls. No crashing of wings.

'I think I'll have another glass of wine,' Kate said as she huddled by the fire. 'Then I deserve a nice long nap.'

Anna put another log on the fire as her mother settled down in an armchair. The fire roared and the beat of the Dragon's heart began. The blood drummed in Anna's ears. Smoke belched from under the floorboards. A tongue of flame flicked high into the air.

'Please go away!' Anna pleaded. The

pounding of blood filled her head now. 'I've told Mum to leave you alone, but she doesn't understand.'

The empty glass slipped from Kate's hand as she dozed into an even deeper sleep. She thought she heard her daughter speaking, but was too tired to answer. The tapping at the door did not wake her. Nor did the calling of the dead.

'You have to leave now!' Grace Palmer screamed, as Anna unbolted the door and Sam raced out into the night. 'The fire's about to start!'

'What fire?' Anna said, puzzled, as she looked back into the hallway. 'I don't understand.'

'Get your mother!' Grace insisted, pushing Anna back into the house. 'She'll burn with the Dragon if you don't go now.'

The Dragon's heart was beating faster

and faster as Anna ran into the front room. The fire was burning fiercely and a shower of sparks burst into the room like fireworks. The straw on the hearthrug caught first, then the dry leaves.

The torn photographs flared up in a sprinkle of fire and burned. A curl of flame caught the pile of catalogues and fabric samples. The wine glass cracked and splintered in the heat.

'Mum!' Anna yelled, as a rocket of flame shot across the room. 'Wake up! We've got to get out.'

There was a loud whooshing like a dragon's breath as the fire spread. Kate staggered to her feet as Anna pulled her from the chair. A line of fire was snaking across the floor as they stumbled towards the door.

'Quickly!' Anna shouted. Now the fire

snatched at the hem of the curtains and roared up to ceiling height. 'Try not to breathe in the smoke.'

The room exploded into a ball of flames as Anna dragged her mother through the smoke-filled hallway. The smoke was thick and black. It was impossible to see and the stench of burning flesh was everywhere.

As Anna coughed and struggled for breath, she felt a hand on her shoulder. The hand was cold in spite of the heat of the fire. Suddenly a smell of mothballs mixed with the smoke.

'This way, Anna,' the old woman's voice said gently. 'Head for the bright light in the distance.'

Then the light disappeared as the ceiling collapsed above their heads, in a thunderbolt of plaster and flames.

THIRTEEN

Kate stared at the burning building as she hugged Anna tightly.

Somehow they had made it through the smoke and into the garden. It was dusk and yet there was a golden light filling the sky. Flames shot out through broken windows like shooting stars. The shutters flapped madly until they cracked and burned.

The Dragon twisted and roared as the roof tiles singed and dropped to the ground like dead scales. It snapped its jaws as its lamp-like eyes exploded in the terrible heat. It put out its claws in agony and burned like a living thing.

Dragon House breathed out smoke for the last time, as its body crashed to the ground.

'It called them home, Mum,' Anna whispered. She saw the pale look of horror on her mother's face.

'The house called them back, the sleeping and the dead. It was the only way it could stop you. Dragon House didn't want to change. It just wanted to sleep.'

'I heard roaring and screaming,' Kate said, holding Anna's cold hand to stop her own from shaking. 'There was a smell of burning skin and bone. Something died in that house, didn't it? Some kind of creature?'

'They called it Dragon House,' Anna replied. 'You know what died.'

FOURTEEN

'I don't suppose they'll ever discover the cause of the fire at Dragon House,' the estate agent said, as he stepped over a pile of ashes and broken glass. 'There was nothing left by the time the fire brigade arrived.'

'Well, it had nothing to do with Morris and Sons!' a man wearing a hard yellow hat replied. 'My lads are skilled builders. If you ask me the fire was caused by faulty wires.'

'The mother and daughter didn't stand a chance,' the estate agent continued. 'It must have been a grim sight when the firemen found their bodies under the rubble. But life goes on. How much are you thinking of offering for the plot of land?'

Mr Morris grinned as he looked at the large, blackened space in front of him. There would be enough room to build at least three small houses on the site of Dragon House.

'I think Morris and Sons will be offering a fair price,' the builder replied. 'We'll have the new houses built and sold by Christmas.'

'Never wake a sleeping dragon, dear,' said a voice behind what was left of the garden gate. 'That wouldn't be wise.'

The two men shivered, in spite of the sunshine. They turned to look into an old woman's grey eyes.

'There's more to life than making money,' the woman added.

'And there's more to death too. Much more … '